We dedicate this book to Asher,
our silly and sweet inspiration,
and to our hero, Seymour Chwast
—S. L. & R. L.

Dedicated to Vicki, Kellie,
and their Silly Babies!
—A. S.

Book design by Katie Jennings.
Typeset in Cheddar Salad.
The illustrations in this book were rendered with oil on gesso board with cat prints.
Manufactured in Hong Kong.

Library of Congress Cataloging-in-Publication Data
Lorig, Steffanie.
Such a silly baby! / by Steffanie and Richard Lorig ; illustrated by Amanda Shepherd.
p. cm.
Summary: Rhyming text and illustrations follow the adventures of a baby who on
excursions to the zoo, the circus, or the farm manages to get switched with an animal.
ISBN 978-0-8118-5134-3
[1. Babies—Fiction. 2. Animals—Fiction. 3. Humorous stories. 4. Stories in rhyme.]
I. Lorig, Richard. II. Shepherd, Amanda, ill. III. Title.
PZ8.3.L886Suc 2008
[E]—dc22
2007013135

10 9 8 7 6 5 4 3 2 1

Chronicle Books LLC
680 Second Street, San Francisco, California 94107

www.chroniclekids.com

Such a Silly Baby!

By Steffanie & Richard Lorig

Illustrated by Amanda Shepherd

chronicle books · san francisco

I went to the zoo
with my li'l baby.
We strolled around
'til after three.

But there was a hitch...

my baby got switched,

and I went home with a chimpanzee.

Well, I went back the very next day.
I found my baby right away.
I switched him with the chimpanzee,
and this is what he said to me:

I'm such a silly baby!

The circus came, I took him there.

We laughed at clowns
with funny hair.

But there was a hitch...

my baby got switched,

and I went home with a dancing bear!

Well, I went back the very next day.
I found my baby right away.
There he was in the center ring,
and this is what I heard him sing:

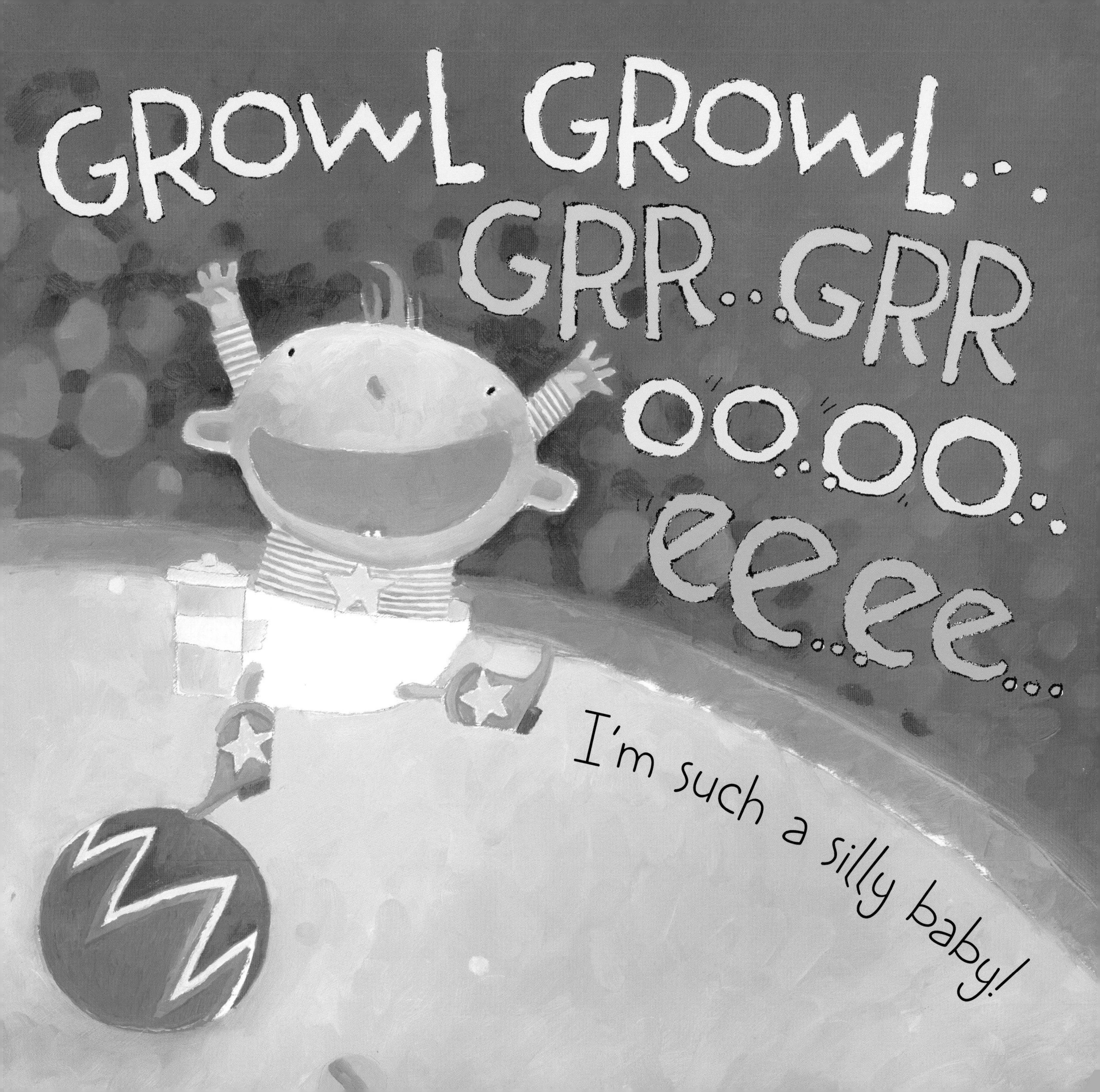

I'm such a silly baby!

Down on the farm
we rode a plow.
And fed grain to
the Jersey cow.

But there was a hitch...

my baby got switched,

and I went home
with a lazy sow.

Well, I went back the very next day.
I found my baby right away.
Oh, where do you think my boy was found?
Rolling with pigs on the muddy ground.

We went to see a Wild West show,
and how this happened I don't know,
but there was a hitch...

my baby got switched,

and I went home with
a buffalo!

Well, I went back the very next day.
I found my baby right away.
My babe was pleased as he could be,
and this is what he said to me:

YEE HAW SNORT SNORT
OINK OINK wee wee
GROWL GROWL...
GRR..GRR
oo..oo..eeee

I'm such a silly baby!

I brought my baby home with me.
He really needed sleep, you see.

But there was a hitch...
Oh, not another switch!?

What do you think
I turned to see?

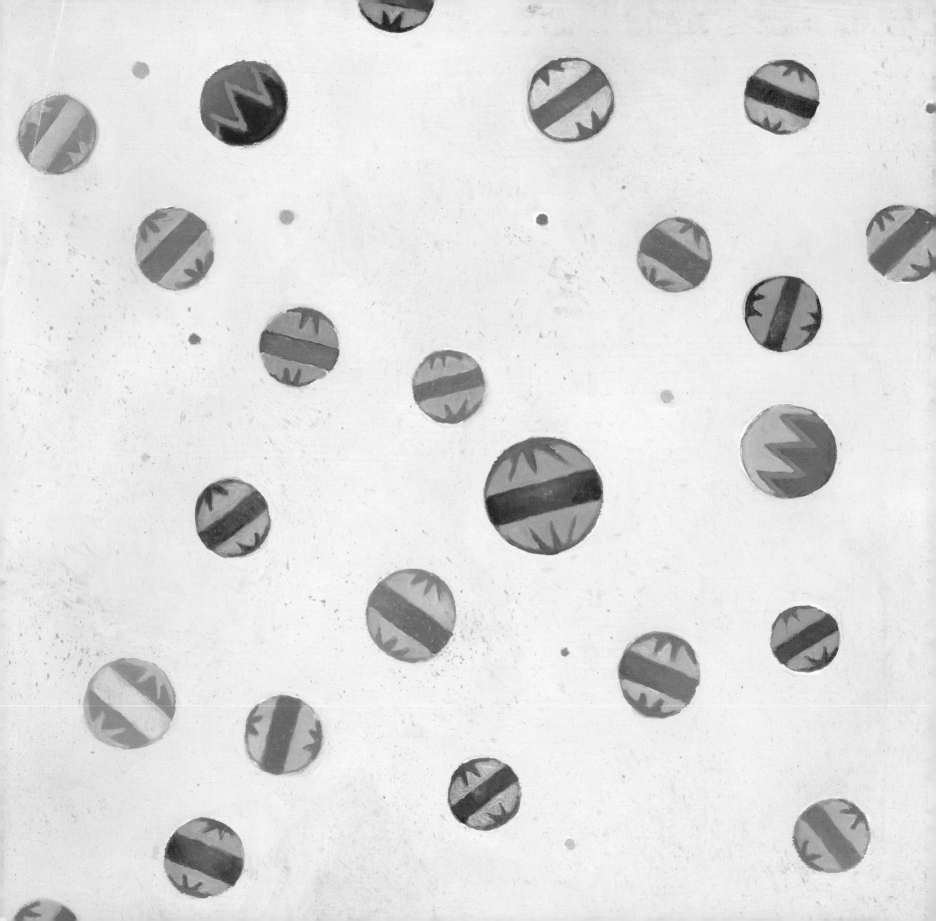